Zia

Loud, confident and intrepid. She's a born leader but can sometimes get carried away. Likes schoolwork and wants to be a scientist when she's older, just like her mum.

Luca

The newest member of the club. He's shy, like his cousin Cassie, but not when it comes to going on an adventure. Is obsessed with watching nature programmes.

Thunder

Big, white and fluffy with grey ears, paws and tail. He's blind in one eye, but that's what makes him extra special. Likes chasing mice, climbing trees and going on adventures. Is also a cat.

Join the friends on
all their Playdate Adventures

THE SECRET JUNGLE HIDEAWAY

★ THE PLAYDATE ★
ADVENTURES

Book Eight

THE SECRET JUNGLE

HIDEAWAY

Emma Beswetherick

Illustrated by Anna Woodbine

ROCK THE BOAT

A Rock the Boat Book

First published by Rock the Boat,
an imprint of Oneworld Publications, 2023

ISBN 978-0-86154-342-7 (paperback)
ISBN 978-0-86154-343-4 (ebook)

Printed and bound in Great Britain by Clays Ltd, Elcograf S.p.A.

Oneworld Publications
10 Bloomsbury Street, London, WC1B 3SR, England

Stay up to date with the latest books,
special offers, and exclusive content from
Rock the Boat with our newsletter

Sign up on our website
rocktheboatbooks.com

To my husband and kids,
for the animal adventures we've had
and the animal adventures still to come

And to my cat Kion, aka Thunder,
for being a true inspiration.
You will forever be in our hearts

CHAPTER ONE

"Finished," Luca's mum announced as she hammered the final nail into the tree-house ladder.

Luca stood back, admiring their creation. The ladder climbed steeply, disappearing every now and then into the dense canopy of leaves above. The tree house itself had enough room for five or six children Luca's size. It wasn't neat – the planks of wood they'd used were wonky, the angles between the joins rarely the same – but to Luca it felt better than perfect.

"So, what do you think?" his mum asked, a hopeful smile on her face.

"Only that it's the c-coolest tree house in the h-history of tree houses!" Luca threw his arms around her, grinning wildly.

"Just the sign to go up now," she said, loading her tools back into her bag. "Here, I'll leave the hammer out for you. I'd better go and get snacks ready for when your friends arrive."

Luca watched his mum disappear into the house, then looked back at the tree house they'd built together over the last few months. They'd collected bits of wood from builders' merchants and scrapyards, and spent every spare evening in the garden, sawing, sanding and hammering pieces into place, determined to finish it by the end of term.

Luca crouched down and picked up the final sign he'd painted over the weekend.

TOP SECRET

PLAYDATE ADVENTURE CLUB
MEMBERS ONLY

Holding the sign against the side of the ladder, he pressed a nail to the middle, then grabbed the hammer and started hitting.

One…two…three strikes and the sign was secure.

Now the tree house was ready. And just in time, because Cassandra, Katy and Zia came charging out into the garden.

"Luca!" Cassandra cried, flinging one arm around her cousin's shoulder. "Auntie's just told us about the tree house!" Cassandra was Luca's cousin first and best friend second. "I can't believe you finished it in time for the holidays!"

Luca grinned and pointed to the ladder. They craned their necks towards the sky.

"That's so cool," enthused Katy, high-fiving Luca in the air. "I've *always* wanted a tree house."

"Is it safe to go up?" Zia asked excitedly.

"Mum says it c-could hold an e-elephant if we wanted it to. So y-yeah." He nodded. "I guess it's r-ready."

Luca had a stammer, which upset him more than he let on. It was his biggest wish to be able to speak without getting stuck on a word. Luckily, none of his friends seemed to mind and always waited patiently for him to finish talking.

"Who w-wants to go first?" he asked.

Zia let out a "WHOOP!" and sprinted over to the ladder. "Last one up's a squashed banana!"

Cassandra and Katy eyed each other challengingly, then raced after Zia. Luca followed closely behind, happy his friends were as excited about his tree house as he was.

The ladder ran up the twisted trunk of the large beech tree, rising through its thick canopy of leaves and branches before arriving at the tree house at the top. Luca watched his three friends climb up onto a platform, then through the crooked doorway before he, too, joined them inside. They were standing with their eyes wide and jaws touching the floor.

"I can't believe how awesome this is!" Cassandra turned and grabbed her cousin's hands, squeezing them tight.

"You really built this?" asked Zia, spinning around.

Luca nodded. "With my m-mum. She's an engineer and usually designs s-skyscrapers in the city, so this w-was easy for her."

Looking at the inside of the tree house now, Luca tried seeing it through his friends' eyes. The main floor space was huge – at least big enough for them to spread their arms out without touching each other. There was a raised platform to one side with a lookout over the allotments beyond the garden fence.

A huge wooden chest sat against another wall, filled with useful things for an adventure, and on 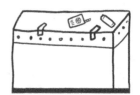 the floor beneath them was a large fluffy rug to make sitting down more comfortable. Above their heads was a roof with beams in different shapes and sizes, and hanging from one window was a pulley with a bucket attached, so anyone in the garden could pass things up from below, and anyone inside could lower things down from above.

"You can see the whole world from up here!" Katy exclaimed, climbing onto the raised platform to peer out of the window.

"Perhaps we should stop being adventurers and start being spies instead," giggled Cassandra. She joined Katy on the platform. "Look, there's Mr Rasheed from school. I never knew he lived around here."

"And *I* never knew he wore shorts during the holidays!" Katy said, grinning. Everyone laughed, until Katy looked thoughtfully at Cassandra. "Actually, I'm never going to stop being an adventurer. It's the best thing I've ever done."

"I'm not sure when our next adventure will be after today, though," said Luca, sighing.

"I know. I'm off to India next week to stay with family for a month," explained Zia.

"And Luca and I are visiting Grandma in Jamaica," said Cassandra.

"Then we need to make this playdate extra special!" Zia exclaimed. "Has anyone thought what our adventure could be today?"

Zia, Luca, Katy and Cassandra were in a top-secret adventure club that not even their parents knew about. Every time they had a playdate, some incredible form of magic turned their imaginary adventures into real ones. Luca was the newest member of the club, and this was the first time he'd had them all round to play. He hoped more than *anything* the magic still worked in his garden. He didn't want to let his friends down.

"Not yet," he replied. "Although a t-tree-house adventure could be f-fun."

"I have an idea," said Katy quietly. She was kneeling and pulling open her backpack. "You know my dad adopted a Sumatran tiger for me for my birthday? I've just been sent the adoption pack, and look –" she smiled, holding out a stiff piece of paper, "– this is my certificate. And this –" she grinned, pulling a soft, cuddly toy from her bag, "– is Nadira. My adopted tiger!"

"Cute!" Cassandra squealed, reaching out to stroke the tiger's head.

"*Really* cute," agreed Zia. "But what's it got to do with our adventure?"

Katy rummaged further in her bag and pulled out a small booklet. She flicked through the pages until she found the one she was looking for. "It says here that Nadira is one of the last Sumatran tigers to live in her part of the jungle. Her coat is darker than other tigers and her stripes are closer together too. You know Sumatran tigers are one of the most critically endangered species in the world? Nadira was raised in captivity, so she's used to humans. I thought we could go on an adventure to find her."

CHAPTER TWO

"A tiger adventure sounds b-brilliant!" Luca exclaimed. "I've always wanted to v-visit a jungle."

"Me too," agreed Zia. "And it's good Nadira's a friendly tiger."

"It means we won't get eaten!" Cassandra grinned, climbing back down from the platform.

"Cassie!" cried Zia. "Don't even joke about it!"

Katy laughed, then hopped down to join them. "It's actually one of the reasons Nadira's special. She has to learn how to survive in the jungle so she can breed and have cubs."

"Then I *definitely* think we should look for her," said Cassandra.

"You know, you've changed, Cassie." Zia was staring curiously at her friend. "When we started the Playdate Adventure Club, you were scared of *so many things*. Now I think you could be the bravest of all of us."

"It's because of our motto," said Cassandra, smiling. "That there's safety in numbers. As long as we're together, I know we're always OK."

Katy smiled back. "I'm glad everyone likes the idea of a tiger adventure. Tigers are the most incredible cats. They've always been my favourite—"

But Katy was interrupted by something loud scratching at the doorway. Two grey ears were peeking around the frame, followed by a whiskery face, a big, fluffy white body, four grey paws and, finally, a grey-tipped tail.

"THUNDER!" they exclaimed in unison.

Thunder was Katy's one-eyed rescue cat and important fifth member of the Playdate Adventure Club. He'd been on every adventure with them, and Katy knew the jungle would

be just up his street. He must have
had a mini adventure of his own,
scaling garden fences between her
home and Luca's, and climbing
right up to the tree house.

"I hoped you'd c-come." Luca grinned as
Thunder sauntered over with a cross look on
his face.

"Thunder, you *know* you're my best cat,"
Katy gushed, holding her hand out to stroke
him. "When I said tigers were my favourite, I
was about to say 'favourite *big* cats'. You're still
my favourite *all-time* cat."

Thunder meowed loudly and began brushing
himself against her legs.

"I'm forgiven then?" Katy giggled, as a wisp
of white cat hair drifted past her nostrils.
"*AAAAACHOOOO!*"

Zia grinned. "All the club's here now.

I think we should start planning. Has anyone wondered how we should get to the jungle?"

Everyone thought for a second.

"We could always go with our f-first idea?" said Luca. "You know – a t-tree-house adventure. We could imagine this t-tree house is actually *in* the Sumatran jungle."

"Where *is* the Sumatran jungle?" asked Cassandra.

"It's in Indonesia," explained Katy. "Did you know Sumatra is the sixth largest island in the world?" She turned to Luca. "I think that's a great plan, by the way. When we open our eyes, we could see tropical trees and vines outside the window."

"The birds could turn into parrots!" offered Zia.

"And there could be monkeys and elephants," added Cassandra.

"And t-tigers, of course!" Luca finished, watching as his friends' imaginations took hold. "Come on. Let's p-pack."

He walked over to the wooden chest by the wall and flung open its lid. It contained binoculars and water bottles with neck straps, a magnifying glass, walkie-talkies, a first-aid kit, energy bars. He threw everything into a rucksack and hoisted it onto his back.

"Are we r-ready then?" he asked.

Everyone nodded.

"Then let's close our eyes and imagine the g-garden changing outside the window." Luca paused to allow everyone to think for a moment, eyes squeezed tightly shut. Then they arranged themselves back into a circle, Thunder meowing softly in the middle.

"OK, now r-repeat after me: I wish to go on an adventure."

"*I wish to go on an adventure,*" they all sang together.

Immediately, their bodies began to feel tingly and super-charged with electricity. The hairs on their arms stuck out, their fingers and toes felt prickly. It was like fizzy-drink bubbles were whizzing around their bloodstreams. They felt light as a feather, as though they could float away, up into the sky. Only when their bodies returned to normal did they dare open their eyes.

"OH!" shrieked Zia.

"MY!" squealed Katy.

"GOODNESS!" cried Luca and Cassandra.

They rushed to look through a window. The green canopy around them was growing. Leaves were waving and reaching towards

17

the tree-house walls. Branches morphed into vines that twisted and twined through the trees and plummeted to the ground below. The adventurers backed away from the windows as green tentacle-like limbs crept closer to where they were standing. The air was warming – feeling stickier, more humid. The noises outside were changing too – gentle birdsong became a cacophony of squawks and whistles, broken by the hoots and screeches of monkeys. And was that an elephant trumpeting in the distance?

Finally, the transformation outside the window stopped, so that now there was only a gentle breeze rustling the leaves.

"I don't think we're in Luca's garden anymore," whispered Cassandra.

"And have you seen what we're wearing?" asked Zia, pointing down at their clothes.

They were now dressed in either tropical shirts or T-shirts, with sturdy walking boots on their feet. Even Thunder was wearing a matching hat and necktie with palm trees on them, the deep frown from earlier firmly back on his forehead.

"You don't like your outfit?" Katy asked him.

"I don't know why we always have to dress up," he moaned. "Isn't it enough that I can talk on our adventures?"

Katy giggled. "Stop being a grump." She heaved Thunder into her arms and planted a kiss on the top of his head, which he batted teasingly away with his paw. "Last one down the ladder is even more of a sourpuss than you!"

CHAPTER THREE

They crept over to the doorway and stared out into the treetops. Lush green leaves covered almost every inch of sky, each coated in water droplets that glittered and glistened in the sunlight. Golden rays streamed through the dense branches, illuminating the green canopy and bathing everything it touched in a shimmering golden glow. The jungle trees and plants gave off a sweet, earthy aroma. Around them, the air thrummed with screeches and squawks, as well as the low buzz and rattle of insects.

They'd seen pictures of jungles and rainforests at school during their topic on deforestation and had even painted their own, which still hung proudly on their classroom wall. Luca had also watched dozens of nature documentaries about them. But nothing could have prepared them for being in a real jungle. It was wild and remote. It felt exciting.

"It's so *hot*!" Cassandra sighed, wiping her forehead, where beads of moisture were already forming.

"Here," said Luca, handing out the water bottles. "We should t-take regular sips. We shouldn't w-wait until we're thirsty."

Cassandra took a long gulp, then placed the bottle around her neck. "OK, I'm happy to go first, unless anyone else wants to?" Zia was right – she *had* grown in confidence over their adventures – but going first still didn't come naturally to her. "Unless *you* want to, Thunder? I mean, you are the best at climbing trees."

Thunder looked pleased with the compliment, then ran and jumped out of the doorway without even a second glance.

"Looks like I'm next then," said Cassandra.

"Good luck!" everyone shouted.

Cassandra gave her friends a thumbs up, then took a deep breath as she gripped the handrails. She swivelled round, found her footing on the rungs and slowly began her long descent, feeling very much like Jack must have done when he climbed down his enormous beanstalk. The ground seemed further away than it did in Luca's garden – the ladder must have doubled, no, TRIPLED, in length, she realised. She heard rustling below her, and three brightly coloured parrots flew out of the leaves and disappeared into a

23

neighbouring tree. Further down, a monkey brushed past her head, almost sending her flying, before it grabbed hold of a vine and swung away through the branches.

Finally, Cassandra's feet reached the ground. She stepped away from the ladder, her heart rate battling to return to normal. One by one, her friends came to stand beside her. They were also breathing heavily, cheeks flushed, foreheads slick with sweat. Only Thunder looked unphased by the long climb down.

"E-everyone OK?" Luca asked.

"Is it just me, or did the ladder seem longer than it did on the way up?" panted Katy, fanning her forehead.

"*Way* longer," Cassandra agreed. She was resting her hands on her thighs and leaning over to catch her breath.

"But *way* better," Thunder pronounced, casually licking his paws.

Katy smiled. "You would say that."

"So how do we find your tiger, Katy? Any idea which way we should g-go?" Zia was staring hopefully at her friend.

Katy opened her backpack and took the booklet out again, flicking through the pages to see if she could find any clues. "It just says that Nadira can be found in the depths of the Sumatran jungle. I guess we start walking – and search for tracks?"

The others came and peered over Katy's shoulder. After a few seconds, Zia broke into a grin.

"Look!" she exclaimed. "See that picture? Nadira's drinking water from a river. And in that one!"

Everyone nodded as they saw what Zia was showing them.

"That's clever, Zia," said Luca. "*All* animals need water to survive."

Katy beamed. "So the river *has* to be the best place to start our search!"

They looked around for a path they could take, but all they could see was dense undergrowth.

"It's that way," Thunder announced, pointing nonchalantly past the ladder. "Didn't you notice on the way down? There's a river beyond some rocks over there. But it's a bit of a walk, I'm afraid."

Katy scratched Thunder behind his ears. "I knew this adventure would be perfect for you," she said. "How about you lead the way again?" She took a few sips of water, then poured some into her cupped hand for Thunder to drink. "Let's keep our eyes peeled for any evidence of tiger on the way."

They were just about to head off when there was an almighty clatter from up high. An enormous orange shape burst out of the leaves, swinging down Luca's ladder at such speed the friends didn't even have time to back away. It sprang to the ground and began banging its large hands on the ground, arms swinging like a drummer's. Its teeth were bared, its eyes fierce and wild.

Katy pulled Thunder into her arms and the four friends huddled together, blood draining from their cheeks.

"WHY IS YOUR HOUSE IN MY TREE?" the orangutan bellowed. "THIS IS *MY* HOME! WHY HAVE YOU COME?"

It continued to bang its hands on the ground, and everyone bunched closer, terrified of what it might do next. Thunder, who usually felt the most confident around animals, burrowed his head into Katy's chest. But then Cassandra remembered an angry polar bear called Pila they'd met in the Arctic. Perhaps, like with Pila, they just needed to explain *why* they'd come to the jungle, make the orangutan listen to their story. She took a brave step forwards.

"Please, we don't mean any harm," Cassandra said quietly, swallowing hard.

"SILENCE!" hollered the orangutan. "I DON'T TRUST HUMANS."

Cassandra put her hands up in a surrender. "You can trust us, I promise. We're looking for a tiger."

"TIGERS ARE DISAPPEARING BECAUSE OF HUMANS!" the orangutan

yelled louder. He puffed his chest out and glared angrily at Cassandra.

"B-but n-not b-because of u-us," Luca stammered, coming to stand supportively by his cousin's side. The bumps in his speech always got worse when he was nervous. "I'm s-sorry our t-tree house l-landed in your tree."

Zia was next to step forwards.

"Our friend Katy has adopted a tiger. It's because she *cares* about animals." She turned her head and signalled for Katy to join them. "Katy, why don't you show, er – I'm sorry, we don't know your name."

"VARIK!" shouted the orangutan, but they could tell he was listening now. His voice didn't sound so loud or threatening.

"Why don't you show Varik your adoption pack? Maybe that might help him understand."

Katy placed Thunder on the ground, opened her bag and took out the booklet. Then she flicked to the page with Nadira drinking from the river.

"This is the Sumatran jungle. See," she said, pointing to the photo. She took a few careful steps towards the orangutan. "And this is Nadira. We just want to meet her and check she's OK."

Varik sat down on his large orange bottom, the brows above his tiny eyes furrowing into a frown.

"Is there s-something wrong?" asked Luca, concerned now that they'd done something else to upset the orangutan.

Varik nodded. "But it's a sad story, and I still don't know if I can trust you." He thought for a second, then took a deep breath. "It's been going on for a long time. Not only tigers, but other animals have been disappearing too. Humans are destroying us – either by poaching or cutting down our trees.

As the jungle shrinks, the number of animals decreases, because there isn't enough food or space for us to survive. We've lost elephants, leopards, rhinos. *Orangutans.* So many species already endangered. Now we think we've lost Nadira. She's the last female Sumatran tiger in the jungle, but we haven't seen her in weeks."

Varik rested his giant head in his hands. His eyes looked glassy, like he was about to cry.

"I'm sad because, if Nadira's gone, the Sumatran tiger could be lost for ever."

CHAPTER FOUR

The five friends hung their heads until Varik coughed loudly. He wanted to hear what these humans had to say.

"I'm s-sorry," Luca mumbled, peering guiltily up at the orangutan. *No wonder Varik doesn't trust us*, he thought. *Humans have done some terrible things.*

Katy also looked like she was about to cry. "You know gone means extinct?" She looked at the others. "Like with the sabre-tooth tiger, or the Tasmanian tiger. It's why animal conservation is so important. We need to protect endangered species before they're lost for good."

"There must be *something* we can do?" Zia asked.

Thunder had been silent the whole time, but now he strode forwards and stared up at the orangutan. "We do what we came here to do," he said seriously. "We find Nadira."

"BUT WHAT IF YOU CAN'T?" Varik bellowed again. It was clear he still didn't trust them.

"There's only one way find out," said Katy defiantly. She stuffed her booklet back in her bag. "Thunder's right. If we don't start looking, we'll never know if the last female tiger is alive. Varik, it's been lovely meeting you, but we really must go."

As they readied themselves to leave, Luca rummaged around in his backpack.

"Varik, I'd like you to h-have this," he said, handing the orangutan one of his walkie-talkies.

Varik snatched the tiny gadget in his hands, frowning, and brought it up to his mouth as if to take a bite.

"NO!" shrieked Luca. "N-not like that. Like this," he said gently, holding the other walkie-talkie up to his face. "It's like a radio, see," he said, twizzling the knob on the top so that a red light came on. Varik did the same, until a loud buzzing noise caused him to jump and almost drop it. Luca took a few steps back and hid behind a tree. "K-keep it turned on, and you'll be able to h-hear me talking if we n-need to get hold of you," he said, speaking into the walkie-talkie. "You need to p-press the button on the side to t-talk back to me."

Varik looked confused as Luca's voice rang out through the gadget in his hands.

"Even when we're apart, we can l-let each other know if we f-find anything," Luca continued. "Hopefully, w-we'll have some good news to share soon."

Varik grunted and scratched his head. He was still staring at the strange gadget in his hands and turning it over when Luca came back to join them.

"I'll leave you to it then," Varik huffed. "Good luck finding Nadira." Then he turned his bulky body around and disappeared into the bushes.

They waited until they were alone again before anyone dared to speak.

"Well, that was scary," Zia sighed, letting out a long breath.

"I actually thought he was going to eat us," Cassandra agreed.

"Although I'm pleased we met him," said Katy. "Because now we have an even bigger reason to find Nadira."

They walked in silence for a while, listening to jungle sounds, in awe of the nature around them. There were palm trees and banana trees and ferns and cactuses and other trees they didn't know the names of that were the tallest they'd ever seen.

Luca stopped and pointed up into the canopy. "Do you know the difference between rainforests and jungles?" Everyone shook their heads. "In a r-rainforest, the t-trees are *even* taller than here in the jungle, and the c-canopy is *even* thicker. It means it's h-harder for sunlight to reach the ground, so not as many p-plants grow on the forest floor."

"Really?" Cassandra gasped.

"I can't imagine trees higher than these," Zia agreed, flapping her arms as a huge insect buzzed past and landed on a spiky yellow flower nearby.

Katy remembered another fact about Sumatra. "You know the Sumatran jungle is one of the world's biodiversity hotspots," she said, pausing to smell a flower by her shoulder.

"What does that mean?" asked Cassandra, joining her.

"It means soooooo many plants and creatures call the jungle their home," Katy said. "It's why wildlife organisations are trying to protect it from being destroyed."

"Doesn't the biggest flower in the world grow in Sumatra?" asked Zia, stopping and inspecting a small mark on the ground. Zia's mum was a scientist and she always knew lots of interesting things.

"I think so," said Luca. "It's the r-rafflesia flower, or something like that."

"Bingo." Zia smiled. "It can grow to the size of a giant umbrella. It's also the smelliest flower in the world. It stinks like rotten meat!"

"We should be able to smell it before we see it then," Cassandra laughed, pinching her nose.

Katy giggled, giving the flower beside her one final sniff. "Come on, let's keep looking."

As they pushed deeper into the jungle, their eyes homed in on the ground and bushes around them. They'd arrived during the hotter dry season, but it still rained every day, so the ground was muddy and the leaves glistened with moisture. Luca remembered a documentary he'd seen of a tracker searching for a family of leopards in the African savannah.

"Remember to look for prints or tracks. A b-broken twig or fur s-snagged on a branch could be an important clue too." He crouched down, taking the magnifying glass out of his rucksack so he could inspect a mark in the mud.

"Have you spotted something?" asked Katy hopefully. She'd also picked up a snapped stick and examined it before tossing it back on the floor.

"Not y-yet, no," Luca sighed. "There's a paw print here, but it's way too small to belong to a tiger."

Everyone crouched low to study the ground where Luca was pointing, but all they could see was a small scuff in the mud and a beetle marching past.

"Then let's keep looking for the river," said Zia. "We're bound to find something there."

They continued walking, alert to the sight or sound of water. Every now and then, when the branches and leaves became too thick, Thunder would leap up a tree to look for a good route from above.

"We've been walking for *ages*," Zia moaned. "My feet are getting tired."

"How much further?" called Katy, as Thunder leapt down a small embankment. The others slipped down inelegantly, dirtying their clothes and scraping elbows and legs on tree roots and rough ground.

"Not much," Thunder replied when everyone had caught up with him. "Look, down there."

They peered over the edge of a rocky precipice. The river was winding its way

41

through the jungle at least ten metres below. But as they stared in horror at the sheer drop beneath them, a loud cracking sound in the distance made them look up again. A tree fell crashing to ground beyond the river. As they continued to watch, they could make out machines moving around in a clearing. They saw another tree fall. And another. The jungle was being destroyed before their very eyes.

CHAPTER FIVE

"What's going on?" cried Cassandra. It was too terrible to witness. Even worse than the dying trees they'd seen on their conker adventure. Worse than any environmental issue they'd learned about – because this was happening *right now*, and they couldn't do anything to stop it.

"They must be cutting trees down to grow crops," said Katy angrily. "That clearing will probably become a palm-oil plantation, or something similar."

Cassandra looked startled. "I can see why Varik was mad. It's another reason the jungle needs our protection."

"But don't humans realise cutting down trees destroys the home of so many creatures?" asked Zia.

Luca shook his head. "I'm sure they realise. But p-palm oil makes money – it's f-found in lots of p-products we use every day. Some s-soaps and shampoos. Even chocolate!"

"*Chocolate?!*" Cassandra cried.

"We need to find Nadira," added Katy, "before her home is destroyed for good."

As they were talking, Thunder had disappeared over the edge of the precipice. They crept forwards slowly and watched as he made his way down, leaping between rocky overhangs.

"It's way too steep for us to climb down," whispered Zia, sizing up the long drop.

But Katy spotted a number of vines hanging over the edge of the rock and reaching all the way down to the riverbank. They gave her an idea. "Have any of you abseiled before?"

Cassandra shook her head.

"I've seen it on TV," said Zia.

"You mean we use v-vines to climb down?" asked Luca.

"Exactly," said Katy, tugging one to check it felt secure. She dangled her legs over the edge, then, taking hold of the vine again, she twisted her body round and pushed her feet against the rock face. Carefully, she walked her feet downwards at the same time as her hands moved one below the other along the vine.

"It's not as hard as it looks," she called out. "Just hold on to the vine tightly and walk while you move your hands down. It's easy once you get the hang of it."

It wasn't easy at all, but Katy didn't want her friends to worry. She held her breath as she walked down the cliff face, praying the vine wouldn't snap. Finally, she heard the river gently gurgling as it skipped and danced along the riverbed. One final jump and her feet reached the ground. She breathed a sigh of relief.

The others weren't far behind. Luca landed next, followed closely by Cassandra, then Zia. Thunder was licking his paws and cleaning behind his ears, acting like he'd been waiting for days.

The river stood nearby, twinkling like a sapphire in the sunlight. It was framed by palm trees and bright, colourful flowers, all reflected in its glassy surface.

"It's beautiful!" cried Katy as a parrot swooped past.

"Like our paintings in class," gasped Cassandra.

"Only better. Why would anyone want to destroy a place like this?"

Luca was taking his boots and socks off, dipping his toes into the water before he started wading in up to his knees.

"C-come on!" he yelled. "The water's lovely!"

"It does look the perfect place to cool off," Zia said, smiling and fanning her face with her plait. "Besides, we need some cheering up."

Everyone copied Luca, leaving socks and boots in a messy pile on the bank while they strode out into the shallow river. It was cold rather than freezing, and before long they were splashing and laughing, trying for a moment to block the images they'd seen from their mind. Only Thunder remained on the bank, sulking.

"I hate being wet," Thunder moaned. "Shouldn't we be looking for your tiger?"

"She's not *my* tiger," shrieked Katy, as Zia splashed water in her face. Katy sprayed her back, soaking Cassandra's shorts at the same time. "But we should carry on looking."

They stared up the river, then down. The trees and vegetation on either side looked tricky to navigate, with low branches growing out over the water, interspersed with large rocks and crags. They were all tired of travelling by foot.

"You know, the easiest way to look for Nadira would be to travel *along* the river," said Cassandra, wading back out and sitting on the bank to dry herself. "At swimming club last summer, we had a competition where we had to build a raft to cross the pool. Each team was given planks of wood and rope to tie the wood together. My team didn't win, but I think I can remember how we made it."

"Yes! I actually think that might work," said Zia, turning to face Katy and Luca. They were still up to their knees in water. "You know we're good at building things."

Cassandra pointed towards a small cluster of trees. "We could use branches," she called to the others.

"And the v-vines we've just climbed down – maybe they c-could be used as ropes," Luca called back, walking to join his cousin on the bank.

Thunder sauntered towards the rocks and began chewing and tugging at a vine with his teeth. Eventually, the vine fell away. Then he got to work, stripping it down with claws and teeth, until a pile of thinner vines lay on the ground, perfect for tying.

Katy and Zia also came out of the river and helped scour the ground for logs and branches. The four friends worked in pairs, searching and carrying, until a sizeable pile had formed on the riverbank.

"We need to lay the branches side by side, without gaps," Cassandra explained, showing them what to do.

Everyone pitched in, until they'd formed a large rectangle of branches on the ground.

"Now's the tricky part," Cassandra continued. "Tying them together."

Thunder grabbed one of the thin vines in his mouth and, quickly and deftly, began weaving it in and out of the branches. Katy fastened it at the end in a tight fisherman's knot, then Thunder took another vine, and another, until eventually Katy and the others had knotted all the branches tightly together.

"Just one more thing," said Cassandra. She pointed to a palm tree with roots growing into the banks. "Thunder, do you think you could reach those coconuts? We could use them as floats."

It didn't take long for Thunder to dislodge them. One by one, coconuts plummeted to the ground, liquid spilling out from the inside as they cracked on impact.

"Coconut water!" yelled Cassandra, running and holding a coconut to her mouth to drink. "Our family drinks it in Jamaica. You *have* to try some!"

Katy poured some into the hollow of a rock for Thunder, then everyone picked up a coconut, held a crack to their lips and began to drink long and hard.

It was the sweetest liquid they'd tasted.

"*Mmmmmmmmmm!*" Zia exclaimed, wiping the stickiness from her mouth.

"*Deee*licious!" Katy agreed. "But I thought coconuts were brown and furry?"

"Only when they're old," Cassandra explained. "They're always green when they're young."

When, finally, they'd secured several whole coconuts to each corner of the raft, they stood back, admiring their creation.

"*Now* the raft is ready." Cassandra smiled. "Who wants to test it out?"

CHAPTER SIX

The raft was heavier than it looked. They took a corner each and dragged it unsteadily down to the river's edge. As they pushed it into the water, the coconuts bobbed out to the side and the logs gently rolled over the surface.

"I'll keep it steady while you guys climb on," Cassandra instructed, eager to get going.

One by one, they clambered on board, including Thunder, who seemed satisfied their journey downstream wouldn't involve him getting wet.

Before Cassandra stepped on, she handed Katy a long stick for steering. Then, when they were all sitting down, Katy used the stick to push the raft away from the side. "Keep your eyes peeled for Nadira!" she said, green eyes sparkling with anticipation.

The journey was exactly what they needed after many tiring hours on foot. The raft bobbed along, caught in a gentle current, while the sun beat down, drying their clothes. Thunder curled up on Luca's lap and was soon fast asleep.

"It's like paradise," said Cassandra, lying back and watching a bird with a huge bill swoop down to the water. It soared back up again, a fish dangling from its beak.

They passed a small herd of elephants drinking and spraying water on the bank, a family of monkeys pointing at their raft and laughing as they played cheekily in the trees.

At one point, they spotted an old crocodile basking on some rocks. Cassandra gasped.

"Crocodiles only attack if you g-get close," Luca assured his cousin. "We're s-safe on the raft."

But Katy plunged the large stick in the water anyway and steered them further away from the bank.

"Have you noticed it isn't always me in charge anymore?" asked Zia when the crocodile was out of sight.

"I have." Katy nodded. "Maybe we've all changed during our adventures."

"You've definitely learned it's OK to be scared," Cassandra said, smiling at Zia.

"And you're more comfortable taking the lead," Zia replied.

"How about m-me?" asked Luca.

"You've always fitted in." Katy grinned, squeezing Luca's shoulder. "But you're more confident around us now. I hardly notice your stammer anymore."

It's still there, though, thought Luca sadly. *My stammer's never going away.* But he didn't say that to his friends. It was just nice to know they didn't focus on it all the time.

They'd been so busy chatting, they hadn't noticed the sky darkening above them, or the large rocks now breaking the surface of the water. Thunder half opened his one eye just in time to see a particularly jagged rock looming ahead. He jumped from Luca's lap.

"Look out!" he cried.

Katy plunged the stick in the water and pushed with all her might. The raft surged to the left, but one side of it clipped the rock anyway. They all lurched forwards and scrambled to hang on, just as a clap of thunder boomed in the distance.

"That was close," said Katy. Heavy rain began to pelt down. Suddenly, it was as if the river from earlier had been replaced by a menacing twin. The current quickened, the rocks grew bigger, closer together. The water was churning, frothing and bubbling and turning white. The raft swayed and wobbled as it picked up speed, and Katy knew there was nothing she could do to steer them to safety.

"What do we do?" she screamed. She dropped the stick and bent over Thunder to protect him from getting wet.

Zia coughed, choking on a splash of river water. Cassandra and Luca turned pale.

The river's power was terrifying – a ferocious monster tossing their tiny raft around. They struck one rock, then another, ricocheting downstream like a ball bearing in a pinball machine. Then the raft began to spin, faster and faster, faster and faster.

"Keep h-holding on!" shouted Luca over the roar of the rain and rapids.

The raft tipped one way, then the other, and as coconuts ripped away from the corners, one side of the raft rose up and snapped in half, capsizing them all into the water.

The shock of the cold hit them. The rapids tossed them over and over. Water went up noses, in eyes, ears, mouths. Finally, still fighting the current, their heads surfaced one by one.

Katy looked around in time to see Thunder's

ears disappear again. She dived down, grabbing blindly at the water. Then she felt wet fur and clutched hold of her cat with the tiny bit of strength she had left. She scrambled over slick, slippery rocks, losing her footing, grazing arms and knees, until at last she collapsed onto the wet mud of the riverbank, Thunder a bedraggled heap by her side.

The others continued to be carried down the river, still battered by heavy sheets of rain. The raft was in tatters now, with bits of wood bobbing haphazardly downstream. Luca wasn't sure how much longer he could stay above water. He looked around for the others and spotted his cousin swimming towards a piece of wreckage from the raft, hauling herself over it and using it as a float.

Great idea, cuz, he thought, searching for another piece to climb onto. He saw a large one approaching fast alongside him, a coconut still attached to one corner. He tried to grab it, but it was just out of reach. He made another grab, kicking his legs to propel him forwards. This time, his fingers found vine. He held on tightly, pulled it closer. With one final tug, the piece of raft bashed into his body and he scrambled on top, rolling onto his back and turning his head away from the thunderous sky above.

He lay there, stunned, breathing in and out. But now he was above water, he could see Zia only a few metres away, arms flailing around.

Luca sat up.

"Zia, g-grab hold of my arm!" he yelled, glad his stammer wasn't causing his voice to completely shut down at such a crucial moment.

He paddled as hard as he could to reach her.

Zia swam with all her might, stretching her arm out to grab hold of Luca's hand. She missed once, twice – but then their fingers locked together. Luca tried to pull her up while Zia kicked with her legs, but every time she attempted to climb on, the wood tipped, almost causing Luca to fall in the river too.

"I'll stay in the water," she said numbly, teeth chattering. "Just don't let go of me, OK?"

Luca clung on, until, at last, the river began to slow and quieten. The rain became a drizzle. The sky began to lighten. Finally, Luca spotted a safe place to get out.

"O-over there!" he shouted to Cassandra, paddling with one arm towards the bank and pulling Zia along with the other.

As the three reached the river's edge, they dragged their tired bodies onto a muddy bank. They lay down, breathing hard, grateful for the solid ground beneath them and the warmth on their skin.

"We've lost Katy and Thunder," Cassandra cried, sitting up and looking around. "We can't have drifted far since we lost them. We should turn back." She unscrewed the lid from her water bottle and took a long gulp.

"Can't we rest first?" Zia sighed.

Cassandra and Luca shook their heads.

"No time. We n-need to find them," Luca said, quickly getting to his feet. "I just hope nothing t-terrible's happened."

CHAPTER SEVEN

Katy and Thunder were lying motionless on the riverbank when an elephant's trumpeting sounded through the trees nearby. Thunder opened one eye and got sleepily to his feet. He stretched two paws out in front and arched his back until he realised Katy still hadn't opened her eyes.

He nudged her shoulder with his head. Nothing. He prodded her with his paw. Still nothing.

Thunder clambered onto her tummy and up

towards her shoulder, where he sat down and *MEOWED* loudly into her ear.

Katy's eyelids flickered. Opened. She reached to stroke Thunder's fur while slowly raising herself up to sitting.

"You're OK!" Thunder grinned and Katy pulled him in for a hug.

"Did you see what happened to the others?" she asked, looking around.

Thunder shook his head.

"I can't see them." Katy felt panicked. "They must have been swept further downstream."

As she scrambled to her feet, she noticed a flash of movement out of the corner of one eye. She thought she saw something orange disappear into the shadows of the trees. It was low to the ground. Animal like. Or perhaps she was just seeing things.

"Let's go," she said to Thunder. "If we follow

70

the river, hopefully we'll find the others soon."

The rain was easing and the jungle felt less threatening. No longer were torrents pounding the canopy like a timpani drum. Instead, there was a gentle *tap-tap-tap* as raindrops tickled the leaves and jungle floor.

Thunder was out in front, plotting a safe course through the trees.

"Sorry you got wet," Katy said.

"It's meant to be the dry season," Thunder called back sulkily.

"That doesn't mean it doesn't rain!" Katy smiled, hurrying to catch up with him. "Just that it doesn't rain as much as in the monsoon season." She stopped and sniffed the air. "What's that smell?"

A scent like rotten meat was drifting towards them. Pinching her nose, Katy edged round the base of a prickly palm tree, careful not to get

71

spiked. Then she broke into a grin.

"A Rafflesia flower!"  she shouted, running towards what looked like a giant red sun bursting from the ground. "Remember Zia telling us about them?"

"It smells disgusting," Thunder groaned, putting a paw to his nose.

"But they're really rare," said Katy. She was standing on tiptoes and peering into the flower's mouth-like middle.

"Be careful," warned Thunder. "It might eat you!"

"It's not carnivorous, silly," giggled Katy, carefully feeling the flower's pimply petals. They were thick and waxy – more like the skin of a toad.

Thunder and Katy were still pinching their

noses when the flash of orange appeared again. This time, Katy was certain: an animal was moving through the jungle up ahead.

"Did you see that?" she whispered, pointing.

Thunder nodded. "Do you think it could be Nadira?"

Katy's heart skipped a beat, then, careful not to make a loud sound, they followed the orange shape silently through the trees.

Luca, Cassandra and Zia doubled back through the jungle, keeping the river in their sights the whole time. The journey by foot was longer than by raft and they couldn't ignore the sinking feeling that something bad might have happened to their friends.

At least they *seem to be enjoying themselves*, thought Luca, staring up at the trees where monkeys were shrieking and swinging on vines.

"Do you think Katy and Thunder are looking for us?" asked Zia, stopping to take a bite of her energy bar. Luckily, the wrapper had kept it dry.

"I hope so," said Cassandra. "Because if they are, it means they're both OK."

Luca crossed his fingers. "How much f-further do you think it is to w-where we l-lost them?" he asked, peering ahead through the trees.

"I'm not sure," said Zia.

"It can't be too far," Cassandra said, trying to sound positive.

Colourful flowers were lining the riverbanks now and they could hear rushing water. Did that mean they'd almost reached the rapids? As they ducked to avoid the sharp tips of some palm leaves, there was a sound up ahead.

"Did you hear that?" asked Cassandra, stopping and straining her ears.

74

The sound came again. They all heard it this time.

"Definitely voices," shouted Zia.

The three of them raced forwards with renewed energy, keeping fingers and toes crossed that they'd found their friends.

A baby orangutan with bright orange fur was sitting alone, surrounded by thick vines hanging from branches overhead. It was stroking the vines with its fingers and sobbing quietly.

Katy and Thunder crouched down in a patch of ferns, watching.

"So it's *not* Nadira," Katy sighed.

"Maybe it's lost," Thunder whispered. "I—"

But he was interrupted by a *WHOOSHING* sound coming from the branches directly above the orangutan. One of the vines that, moments before, had been hanging immobile was now moving. It slipped without warning to the ground, then slowly slithered towards the orangutan. At the front were two menacing eyes, a forked tongue. Its mouth was open. It had long, threatening fangs.

"Thunder! Help!" Katy felt desperate. "What do we do?!"

Thunder placed a paw over his eye.

"I know you hate snakes," Katy cried, "but we *need* to do *something*."

Without stopping to think anymore, Katy leapt up from her hiding place and charged ahead with Thunder behind her. She took hold of the orangutan's shoulders and lifted it away from the snake's bite. As soon as she put it down, it ran away as fast as it could. Now the snake turned its hungry attention to Katy and Thunder. Within seconds, its long tail had encircled them.

"*Sssssssssssssssssssssssssupper*," the snake hissed, its narrow tongue flicking in and out. Katy and Thunder could feel the snake's hypnotic stare. Its coils tightened around them: they were both completely trapped.

Katy pulled Thunder into her arms. There was nowhere left for them to run.

"It *is* them!" Zia cried excitedly. "Thunder! Katy! Over here!"

Cassandra looked worried. "Shhhhh," she whispered, tugging at Zia's top. "Katy and Thunder are in trouble."

Luca was frozen to the spot, his face pale with fright.

"Trouble?" whispered Zia. "What do you me—" But she cut herself short when she spotted the snake circling her friends.

"*Sssssssssupper!*" the snake hissed again.

"What do we do?!" whispered Zia, ducking down so they wouldn't be seen.

"We c-can't g-go up against a b-boa constrictor," Luca replied. He knew what they were capable of. They could squeeze the life out of any human even before they swallowed the body whole. He didn't like to think about what a snake this size could do to four children and a cat.

"But we have to save them!" Cassandra cried, choking on her words.

"Snakes are s-stronger than us," Luca explained. "If we g-get too close, it could t-trap us in its coils and we'd all be d-dinner."

Zia took a step back. She looked up at the trees where monkeys were still playing among the vines. A plan was forming in her head. "We need to distract it somehow," she said, thinking things through. "If I stay here, you two could climb that tree and onto those low branches above Katy and Thunder. When I shout and surprise the snake, you could reach down and pull them up to safety. Then I'll climb up into the tree too and we can use the vines to swing away together – just like the monkeys are doing."

Zia looked over at Katy, who was now holding Thunder tightly in her arms. Surely Luca and Cassandra could take Katy and Thunder's weight for a short while?

"I can't think of another plan," Cassandra said, looking anxious.

Luca nodded in agreement before setting off.

Zia watched as her friends crept closer, then clambered up the tree and silently crawled along a thick, outstretched branch towards Katy and Thunder. When they were sitting directly above them, Cassandra gave Zia the thumbs up.

79

Zia burst out from behind the bush, shouting and waving her arms. The snake turned its stare on her, briefly relaxing its coils. At that exact moment, while gripping the branch they were sitting on with their legs, Cassandra and Luca reached down to rescue their friends.

CHAPTER EIGHT

Katy turned when she heard Zia shouting, then immediately felt herself being grabbed under the arms. She and Thunder were hoisted up-up-up and away from the snake's deadly coils. She had no idea how they'd been rescued – until Cassandra and Luca's faces came into view overhead. Thunder scrabbled onto the branch they were sitting on, and Katy was heaved up beside them.

"How did you…? Where have you—"

"No time," interrupted Luca, as a breathless

Zia climbed up to join them. "Follow us. Copy the m-monkeys!"

Within seconds, they were flying through the trees on vines. Like Tarzan of the Apes, they swung and flew, swung and flew, with Thunder swinging alongside. The web of branches and vines formed the most elaborate of treetop playgrounds. The thrill of the ride

helped briefly disguise the terror they'd felt only moments before.

"WOOOOOO-HOOOOOOO!" they all sang out, as they followed the monkeys, flying across a narrow ravine.

The monkeys howled and performed tricks, clearly enjoying the chance to show off to their new audience.

After a while, the vines thinned out until there were no more to swing from. The five friends waved goodbye to the monkeys and lowered themselves to the ground.

"Thank you for saving us!" sobbed Katy, throwing her arms around her friends.

"You don't need to thank us," Zia said, hugging her back. "You would have done the same if we'd been in trouble!"

"But how did you even find us?" Thunder asked.

"We trekked back along the r-riverbank," explained Luca. "Then we h-heard voices."

"We hoped they were yours," Zia added, "so we rushed over. That's when we saw you trapped by the snake."

Katy nodded. "We saw a flash of orange and thought we'd found Nadira. But it turned out to be a baby orangutan who was caught by the snake first. I wonder where it went?"

The monkeys were shrieking and pointing, clearly excited about something in the trees above. The children looked up and saw the baby orangutan swinging in the branches. It landed on the ground by their feet.

"You followed us?" asked Katy, kneeling and reaching out her hand.

The baby orangutan looked uncertain. Then crept a little closer. "You saved me from the snake," it said shyly.

Katy nodded. "You see, we're not here to hurt you. Are you all alone?"

"I've lost my dad," it sighed, finally taking her hand.

"Your dad?" asked Luca.

"His name's Varik," said the baby. "I'm Vishee."

"Varik?" asked Katy. She stared excitedly at the others. "We've met him. It was a long way

87

from here."

Suddenly, Luca's eyes lit up. He opened his backpack and pulled out the walkie-talkie.

"Luca! You're a genius!" Katy shrieked.

Luca smiled and twizzled the knob. But the device was soaking wet. He shook it and drops of water sprayed out. He tried tuning it again – a faint red light came on, then a whirring sound. He held it up to his lips.

"Varik, can you h-hear me? It's Luca. We've f-found Vishee."

There was just the sound of static from the other end.

"Varik, do you c-copy?"

Everyone gathered round, straining to listen through the static. The scratchy sound changed. They thought they heard a voice saying '*hello, hello*'. Then everything went dead.

Luca's shoulders slumped.

"Vishee, how did you lose your dad?" asked Zia.

Vishee shrugged. "We were heading for the hideaway when he disappeared. I've been searching all day."

"The hideaway?" asked Katy.

"It's where endangered species go," Vishee explained. "There aren't many orangutans left in the jungle, so Dad said we should go too. But I don't know where it is."

Katy looked at the others. "Did Varik mention a hideaway?"

They shook their heads.

"Vishee, we've been looking for Nadira," said Cassandra. "We promised Varik we'd try to find her. Maybe you could come with us? We could help you find your dad too."

Vishee nodded. "And I'll help you look for Nadira. She's been lost for weeks."

The monkeys had scarpered now. The jungle felt darker, quieter. As they readied themselves to leave, Luca picked up a stick and started bashing the branches of a nearby tree.

"Who's h-hungry?" he asked.

Everyone looked up as a bunch of bananas fell to the ground. They were sweet and delicious – just what everyone needed before another trek through the jungle.

They stayed close to the river, eating their bananas as they walked, still certain that being near water was their best hope of finding Nadira. The ground was saturated from the rain, and Thunder was dancing around small puddles in the mud.

"I've never been to this part of the jungle," said Vishee, looking around. Huge tree roots had grown overground and formed what looked like an entrance to a cave. Ferns covered the roof in a scratchy green blanket.

"Could that be the hideaway?" asked Katy. But Vishee shook his head.

"Dad says the hideaway's made of gold. We won't find it here."

They carried on walking, but Katy was watching curiously as Thunder put his front paw down in a puddle, lifted it, then put it down again.

"Thunder, what are you doing?" she asked. "I thought you hated getting your feet wet."

But then Luca's eyes popped from their sockets.

"It's not a puddle!" he cried, throwing himself to the ground by Thunder's feet.
"It's a p-paw print, look!"
He didn't need to use his
magnifying glass – the
paw print was huge!

Everyone stared. There were prints forming a zigzag line back towards the cave. They were definitely cat-like – but made by an animal at least five times bigger than Thunder.

"Do you think it could be…?" said Katy.

Her friends nodded excitedly.

They crept over to the cave and peered inside.

CHAPTER NINE

It was dark and cool between the twisted tree roots. Rays of evening sun created a criss-cross of shadows on the walls and floor. A female tiger lay in one corner – surrounded by five tiny cubs.

Everyone grabbed hold of each other's hands and squeezed, their mouths wide open. It was the most incredible sight they'd ever seen.

"Are you Nadira?" Katy asked gently.

The tiger nodded, and everyone's hearts swelled with relief and joy. Then one of the more mischievous cubs wandered over and merrily batted Thunder with its paw. Katy had never seen Thunder so happy to have a playmate!

"We thought you were lost!" Vishee exclaimed, stepping out from behind his new friends.

Nadira raised an eyebrow – she looked tired. Her cubs were scrambling onto her tummy, tugging playfully at her ears and fur.

"You're the tiger I've adopted," said Katy, approaching carefully and kneeling beside her. She opened her backpack and pulled out her certificate. "We've been on quite the journey to find you. Varik said you'd disappeared. I'm so happy you're OK – and that you've had cubs!"

Vishee gave a shy grin. "They found *me* while they were looking for *you*," he announced proudly. "I was looking for my dad when they saved me from a snake!"

Nadira smiled. "You're Varik's son?" Vishee nodded, and she went on. "I was on my way to the hideaway, but these cubs decided to come early so I never made it there. I'm sure that's where your dad will be."

"You know about the hideaway?" Zia asked.

"All endangered species do," said Nadira. "It's the safest place for us.

But it's too far for these cubs to travel." She opened her mouth and yawned, showing razor-sharp teeth. "We'll go when they're bigger."

Katy knew how important it was to get Nadira's cubs to safety. If Nadira was the last remaining female in the jungle, her cubs could be the Sumatran tiger's last hope for survival. "I don't think we should wait," she said, looking concerned. "We've seen where the jungle is being destroyed. It's not far from here."

"Could we help c-carry the cubs?" suggested Luca.

Nadira studied each of their faces. Then she rose sleepily to her feet and stretched the way Thunder did when he got up from a nap. "You're right," she said. "It isn't safe here." She picked up the largest cub with her mouth, holding carefully to the loose bit of skin around its neck. Katy pulled the mischievous one into her arms and stood up. It was the cutest, fluffiest creature – except for Thunder, of course.

Carrying the cubs safely in their arms, the four friends walked with Nadira, Thunder and Vishee by their sides, until the sun had almost set and the sky had turned from blue to pink and orange. When their feet couldn't walk anymore, Nadira stopped. Tall trees with drooping branches had created a gigantic curtain of leaves. There was a tiny opening between, so well camouflaged that anyone who didn't know it was there would walk past unaware.

Nadira lay the cub she was carrying on the ground and pulled the leafy branches back with her teeth. They all walked through the small opening and suddenly the sky felt lighter, the air clearer, the jungle brighter. A golden temple stood before them, glistening brightly like the sun. Intricate spires of various sizes soared majestically into the sky. There were statues of golden animals guarding the doorways – tigers, elephants, rhinos, orangutans – mighty beasts that were vulnerable to the harm humans could wreak on their jungle. This was their safe place. Their secret.

"The hideaway!" Vishee squealed.

"It *is* made from g-gold!" Luca gasped.

They followed Nadira up a steep golden staircase, while Vishee raced to the top and waited by a magnificent doorway. When they stepped inside, they each stood still for a second, marvelling at the sight before them. Golden walls surrounded them, and in the middle was a pool of crystal-clear turquoise water edged by plants and flowers in every colour of the rainbow. Around the pool was a host of jungle animals – rhinos, elephants, bears, monkeys, porcupines, eagles – even a magnificent male tiger. Standing at the back was Varik.

Varik pushed his way to the front and swept Vishee up in his arms. "Son, how did you get here?" he cried. "I was looking for you everywhere!" That's when he noticed Nadira with the four humans and the cat standing by her side. "You found Nadira!"

Katy and the others placed the cubs on the ground. They immediately started rolling around, nipping at each other's ears and tails. "We found these guys too," she said, smiling. "Nadira was on her way here. They're the reason she didn't make it."

"So *that's* why we haven't seen you," he chuckled, looking at Nadira. "Tigers cubs! A very welcome addition to our jungle."

"You know these humans saved me from a snake?" Vishee interrupted, poking his dad's

face to get his attention. All the animals listened as the young orangutan told the story of Katy and Thunder's bravery and how they found Nadira tucked away in the roots of a tree.

Varik smiled again. "Most humans don't care about our jungle. Now, I finally see we can trust you. Thank you for saving my son. And for finding Nadira and her cubs."

"This p-place is incredible," said Luca, looking around in wonder.

Nadira nodded. "You'll find at least one male and female of every endangered species in the jungle here. That way, if our habitat continues to be destroyed, we can save ourselves from extinction."

"But it's top secret," said Varik. "Can you imagine what would happen if its location got into the wrong hands?"

"You mean poachers?" asked Cassandra.

Varik nodded. "Yes, and humans with their machines."

"We've seen the machines," said Katy, sounding worried. "We saw tall, healthy trees falling to the ground. I think the machines are getting closer."

"Don't worry," said Nadira calmly. "This hideaway is special. I promise, we're safe in here, no matter what happens out there."

Zia took a step forward. "We know about the Sumatran tigers, but how endangered are orangutans, Varik?"

"Critically endangered," Varik shot back. "As humans destroy our home, there isn't space for us all to live. We've already lost Vishee's mother. That's why we were on our way here – until I got distracted by your tree house." He smiled. "I thought it might have been another secret hideaway. Or even a trap. I lost Vishee when I climbed down the ladder and found you."

"No wonder you were angry," said Zia.

"Not anymore," said Varik. "You rescued my son!"

"And found Nadira," said Vishee.

"So we can go home knowing the animals are safe." Cassandra smiled warmly at her friends.

"Is it time to say goodbye already?" asked Katy, looking sad.

Nadira nuzzled her head against Katy's legs. "You know we'll always be connected. It means the world to have your support and protection."

Nadira signalled to Varik with a nod. He walked to the back of the hideaway, returning moments later with something in his hand.

"Please accept these as a thank you for everything you've done."

He gave each of them a small stone with an

engraving of a tiger's paw print on its surface.

"Thank you!" everyone sang out.

Luca threw his arms around the orangutan. "I p-promise we won't forget you," he said. "And we'll never reveal your h-hiding place."

"But we *will* tell people how important it is to protect endangered species," said Katy. "By adopting animals and helping to preserve your habitat."

Cassandra and Zia nodded and gave her hands a squeeze.

They said their final goodbyes, Varik wrapping everyone in his long arms. Then they positioned themselves in a circle, Thunder in the middle, and closed their eyes.

"Repeat after me," instructed Luca, "I w-wish to go home."

"*I wish to go home,*" they chanted together.

They imagined Luca's tree house, the

allotments beyond the garden fence, his mum making snacks in the kitchen. Immediately, fizzing sensations whizzed through their bodies. This time, the hideaway began to vibrate as well, the world around them becoming hazy, altering in shape, changing in feel. Only when the sensations had stopped completely did anyone dare to open their eyes.

They were back in ordinary clothes and standing on the rug inside Luca's tree house. Luca hopped onto the platform and gazed outside.

"My garden!" he cried. "And the allotments!"

Thunder meowed as he pushed something around with his paw. It was Katy's cuddly tiger.

"Nadira said we'd always be connected." Katy smiled and bent down to pick the tiger up, holding it tightly to her chest.

"I'm so glad we found her," said Zia.

"And I'm so happy she's had cubs," said Cassandra, "because now there's hope for her species." She reached out to stroke the tiger's head.

That's when they noticed the charm bracelet on Cassandra's wrist. They'd collected a charm on every magical playdate they'd been on. Now a tiny silver paw print hung next to the crescent moon they'd collected on their last adventure. The bracelet looked perfectly complete.

"Eight charms for eight playdate adventures." Zia smiled.

"I'll never forget what we've learned," said Cassandra.

"Or what amazing f-friends you are," said Luca.

Thunder meowed.

"Including you, Thunder!" said Katy, and everyone giggled.

107

"To friendship!" Luca exclaimed, gathering everyone for a group hug. "And to s-saving the planet, one adventure at a time!"

**How to Plan Your Own
Playdate Adventure**

1. Decide where you would like to go on your adventure.

2. Plan how you would get there. Do you need to build anything or imagine yourself in a new land?

3. Imagine what exciting or challenging things might happen on your adventure.

4. Try to learn something new from your adventure.

5. Most important of all, remember to have fun!

ENDANGERED SPECIES

Did you know…?

Today, around one million animal and plant species are threatened with extinction.

The Sumatran tiger is one of the most critically endangered species of tiger, with fewer than 400 remaining. Ninety-five per cent of wild tigers have been lost in the last century, with the Bali, Caspian and Javan tigers already extinct.

On average, 2,000–3,000 orangutans die every year. Without projects to protect them, orangutans could be extinct in the wild in less than fifty years.

Sumatran rhinos are the only Asian rhinos and the most threatened rhino species on the planet.

In Africa, around fifty elephants are killed each day, primarily by poachers for the illegal ivory trade. That's 20,000 a year. Asian elephants are also endangered, with the Sumatran elephant classified as critically endangered.

The world's biggest flower, the rafflesia flower, once thrived in rainforests and jungles, but is now in danger of extinction due to its buds being harvested and sold for medical purposes.

Human beings pose the greatest threat to the survival of endangered species, with poaching, habitat destruction and the catastrophic effects of climate change the primary causes.

In the Sumatran jungle, the biggest threat comes from poaching, illegal logging and deforestation due to the growth of palm-oil plantations. Palm oil can be found in many household products, such as shampoo, soap and chocolate spread, so always try to buy products that are palm-oil free.

The good news is, there are many things we can do to turn the fortunes of these animals and plants around:

Support one of the many organisations that fight to save endangered species. You could even adopt an animal, just like Katy! A full list of animals for adoption can be found on the WWF website: wwf.org.uk. The money raised will go to help protect some of the world's most vulnerable animals.

🍃 Raise money for an animal conservation charity by coming up with your own fundraising ideas.

🍃 Reduce, re-use and recycle more.

🍃 Do all you can to conserve water.

🍃 Try to buy products that are environmentally friendly – and palm-oil free!

🍃 Reduce the amount of meat you eat, which in turn will help reduce the vast areas of rainforest and jungle being cleared for cattle farming.

🍃 Don't buy products made from ivory.

🍃 Learn more about animal conservation and help to spread the word!

Emma Beswetherick is the mother of two young children and wanted to write exciting, inspirational and enabling adventure stories to share with them. Emma works in publishing and lives in south-west London with her family and two ragdoll cats, one of whom was the inspiration for Thunder. *The Secret Jungle Hideaway* is her eighth book.

Find her at: emmabeswetherick.com

Anna Woodbine is an independent book designer and illustrator based in the hills near Bath. She works on all sorts of book covers from children's to adult's, classics to crime, memoirs to meditation. She takes her tea with a dash of milk (Earl Grey, always), loves the wind in her face, comfortable shoes and that lovely damp smell after it's rained.

Find her at: thewoodbineworkshop.co.uk

JOIN THE CONVERSATION ONLINE!

Follow us for a behind-the-scenes
look at our books. There'll be exclusive
content and giveaways galore!
You can access learning resources here:
oneworld-publications.com/rtb
Find us on YouTube
as Oneworld Publications
or on Facebook @oneworldpublications
or on Twitter and Instagram as
@Rocktheboatnews

Nelson Thornes

First published in 2007 by Cengage Learning Australia
www.cengage.com.au

This edition published under the imprint of Nelson Thornes Ltd,
Delta Place, 27 Bath Road, Cheltenham, United Kingdom, GL53 7TH

10 9 8 7 6 5 4 3 2
11 10 09 08

A Night Out
ISBN 978-1-4085-0063-7

Story by Carmel Reilly
Illustrations by Kate Ashforth
Edited by Kate McGough
Designed by James Lowe
Series Design by James Lowe
Production Controller Emma Hayes
Audio recordings by Juliet Hill, Picture Start
Spoken by Matthew King and Abbe Holmes
Printed in China by 1010 Printing International Ltd

Website www.nelsonthornes.com

A Night Out

Carmel Reilly   Kate Ashforth

Contents

Friday Night

It was Friday night.
Raf's mum took Raf and his friend Ruby
to the school dance.

"I'll come back and get you at nine,"
Mum said.
"Have fun!"

Raf and Ruby walked into the school hall.
There were a lot of kids inside.

There were kids
in big groups
and kids
in little groups.

Some were laughing
and shouting
over the music.
Some were eating and drinking.

But no one was dancing.

Ruby wanted to dance.

She grabbed Raf's hand and took him out into the middle of the room.

Chapter 2

No One Is Dancing

Some boys shouted out to Raf.
He did not hear what they said,
but they looked like
they were laughing at him.

8

Raf looked at Ruby and shook his head.

"No, Ruby," he said.
"I don't want to dance now."
Raf walked away.

Ruby looked over at the boys.
"Don't think about them," she said.

Raf shook his head again.
"Look! No one is dancing!" he said.

Ruby gave Raf a funny look.
"Oh, Raf!" she said.

"I don't want to be alone out there,"
Raf said.

"You will not be alone!
I'll be with you.
It will be fun," said Ruby.
"But you will not have fun
if you don't dance."

Ruby started dancing.
She did not look at the boys.
She was getting into the music.
She was having a fun time.

Raf started dancing, too.
He did not look at the boys.
He did not think about them.
He did just what he wanted to do.

13

Chapter 3

Not Alone

Raf was starting to have fun
when he bumped into something.
He stopped and looked around.

He wanted to laugh.
He and Ruby were not alone now.
All the kids were coming over
to dance with them.

The boys were dancing, too.
They were all having fun.
No one was looking at Raf.

Raf's mum came back at nine.

"Did you have a good night?"
Mum said as they got into the car.

"We danced a lot," said Ruby.

"It was good fun," said Raf, laughing.
"Really good fun."